# Karen's Leprechaun

**Look for these**
**and other books about Karen**
**in the**
**Baby-sitters Little Sister series**

# BABY-SITTERS
## Little Sister

# Karen's Leprechaun
## Ann M. Martin

Illustrations by Susan Tang

A
**LITTLE APPLE**
PAPERBACK

SCHOLASTIC INC.
New York Toronto London Auckland Sydney

ISBN 0-590-48231-9

12 11 10 9 8 7 6 5 4 3 2 1          5 6 7 8 9/9 0/0

Printed in the U.S.A.                    40

First Scholastic printing, March 1995

*The author gratefully acknowledges*
*Stephanie Calmenson*
*for her help*
*with this book.*

# Karen's Leprechaun

# 1

# Follow-the-Leader

"It is my turn to be the leader!" I said.

My friends and I were playing follow-the-leader in front of the little house. I have two houses — I have a little house and a big house. (I will tell you about them later.)

"Can we play with you?" asked Andrew. Andrew is my little brother. He is four going on five. He was with his friend, Alicia.

"Okay, come on," I replied.

I am Karen Brewer. I am seven years old. I have blonde hair, blue eyes, and a bunch of freckles. I wear glasses. I even have two pairs. My blue pair is for reading. My pink pair is for the rest of the time. Oh, yes. There is something else you should know about me. I *love* being the leader.

"Ready, everyone? Follow me!" I called.

I held my arms up in the air. I spread out my fingers and curled them forward like claws.

"Roar! Roar!" I shouted.

It was a cold March day. My teacher, Ms. Colman, told us that March comes in like a lion and goes out like a lamb. That is why I was making believe I was a lion.

"Roar! Roar!" called Bobby Gianelli. Bobby lives on my street. He is also in my class at school. I used to think he was a bully. But he is not so much of a bully anymore. We are friends most of the time.

"Roar! Roar! This is fun," said Nancy. Nancy Dawes is one of my two best friends. She lives next door to the little house. (My other best friend is Hannie Papadakis. She lives across the street from the big house.

My two friends and I are in the same second-grade class at school. We call ourselves the Three Musketeers.)

Kathryn Barnes was roaring behind Nancy. Willie Barnes was roaring behind Kathryn. Kathryn is six. Willie is five. They are sister and brother. They live across the street from the little house.

Then came Andrew. Behind him was Alicia. I already told you that Andrew is my brother. Alicia is Bobby's sister. She is four.

We marched up and down the street roaring like scary lions. Then it was Bobby's turn to be the leader.

"Let's have a parade," he said. "It is almost time for St. Patrick's Day." (There will be a real parade in Stoneybrook then.) "I am going to be the leader of the band. Everyone follow me."

We all lined up behind Bobby. We made believe we were playing musical instruments.

*"Boom, boom, boom-boom-boom!"* I said. I

was beating on my make-believe drum.

"Karen! Andrew! Time for lunch," called Mommy.

"We will be right there," I replied.

I beat my make-believe drum a few more times. Andrew tooted a few more times on his make-believe flute.

"See you later," I said to my friends. Then Andrew and I ran inside for lunch.

# Being a Two-Two

I promised to tell you the story of my two houses. Are you ready? Here it is.

First of all, I used to live in only one house. That was when I was little. I lived with Mommy, Daddy, and Andrew in a big house in Stoneybrook, Connecticut. Then Mommy and Daddy started to fight a lot. They tried to work things out so they would not fight so much. But they just could not do it. They told Andrew and me that they love us very much. But they did not love each other anymore. So they got a divorce.

Mommy moved with my brother and me to a little house in Stoneybrook, Connecticut. Daddy stayed at the big house. (It is the house he grew up in.) Now Andrew and I live at the little house for one month. The next month we switch and live at the big house. And so on all year long.

After the divorce Mommy met Seth. They got married. That makes Seth my stepfather. So the people who live at the little house are Andrew, Mommy, Seth, and me. There are some pets, too. They are Rocky, Seth's cat; Midgie, Seth's dog; Emily Junior, my rat; and Bob, Andrew's hermit crab.

Daddy met someone new after the divorce, too. Her name is Elizabeth. She and Daddy got married. That makes Elizabeth my stepmother. She was married once before and she has four children. They are my stepbrothers and stepsister. Here are the people who live at the big house: Andrew; me; Daddy; Elizabeth; David Michael, who is seven like me; Kristy, who is thirteen and the best stepsister ever; Sam and Charlie, who are so old they are in high school. Plus I have an adopted sister. Her name is Emily Michelle. She is two and a half. Daddy and Elizabeth adopted Emily from a faraway country called Vietnam. (I love Emily. That is why I named my rat after her.)

Wait. There is one more person living at the big house. Nannie is Elizabeth's mother. That makes her my stepgrandmother. She came to live at the big house when Daddy and Elizabeth brought Emily home. She helps take care of Emily and everyone else.

Now I will tell you about the pets at the big house. They are Shannon, David Michael's big Bernese mountain dog puppy; Boo-Boo, Daddy's cranky old cat; Crystal Light the second, my goldfish; Goldfishie, Andrew's you-know-what; and Emily Junior and Bob, who live wherever Andrew and I are living.

I have a special nickname for Andrew and me. I call us Andrew Two-Two and Karen Two-Two. (I got that name from a book Ms. Colman read to my class. It is called *Jacob Two-Two Meets the Hooded Fang*.) I call us those names because we have two of so many things. We have two houses, two families, two cats, and two dogs. We have two sets of clothes and toys and books. (That makes it easier for us to go back and forth between our houses. We do not have to pack much each time.) And I already told you about my two best friends, Hannie and Nancy.

Wow! I have two of a lot of things. Sometimes being a two-two is hard. But most of the time I like it. After all I have two families to love me. What could be bad about that?

# An Invitation

"Mmm. That smells really good," I said.

It was Friday afternoon. I had followed my nose into the kitchen. Mommy was at the stove stirring something in a big pot.

"I made some chicken soup," said Mommy. "I am glad you are here. I would like you and Andrew to take some over to the Dawses and the Druckers."

Goody. Delivering soup is an important job. I like important jobs. I ran upstairs to get Andrew. He was in his room reading a book. (Did you know that I helped Andrew learn to read? Well, I did.)

"Come on, Andrew," I said. "We have a job to do."

It was chilly outside. So Andrew and I put on our warm jackets, our hats, and our mittens. Mommy handed us each a small shopping bag with a container of chicken soup.

"You can stop and visit if you like. Just be home in time for dinner," Mommy said.

*Ding-dong.* We rang Nancy's bell first. I knew that Nancy and her mommy were out buying shoes. But Mr. Dawes was home.

"Hi, Karen. Hi, Andrew," said Mr. Dawes.

"Mommy asked us to bring you this soup," I said.

"It is chicken soup," said Andrew.

"What a nice surprise," said Mr. Dawes. "Thank you very much."

"You are very welcome," I said. "Say hi to Nancy."

The next stop was the Druckers' house.

The Druckers live down the street.

*Ding-dong.* Mr. Drucker came to the door.

"Hi, Mr. Drucker," I said. "We have some soup for you. Mommy made it and asked us to bring it over."

"It is chicken soup," said Andrew.

"Chicken soup on a chilly day. What could be nicer than that?" said Mr. Drucker.

"Hello, children," said Mrs. Drucker. "Would you like to come in and visit? We would love the company."

"Sure," I replied. "We just have to be home in time for dinner."

Mrs. Drucker brought out a tray of apple juice and some cookies. Mr. Drucker told us about his garden club. They call themselves the Green Thumbs. That is almost as good a name as the Three Musketeers.

"We are going to ride on a float in the St. Patrick's Day parade. We will all be dressed in green plant costumes," said Mr. Drucker.

"Each member of the club can invite their children or grandchildren to wear costumes

and ride on the float with them," said Mrs. Drucker. She looked sad when she told us that.

"Unfortunately, our grandchildren cannot come. They live too far away," said Mr. Drucker.

"That is too bad for them. Wearing a costume and riding on a float sounds like fun," I said.

Mr. and Mrs. Drucker looked at each other. Then they looked back at Andrew and me.

"Since our grandchildren cannot come, perhaps you and Andrew would ride on the float with us," said Mrs. Drucker.

"Wow! That would be so cool!" I said.

"We better ask Mommy," said Andrew.

Mr. and Mrs. Drucker let us use their phone. Guess what. Mommy said yes!

The Druckers were so happy. Andrew and I were happy, too. We were going to be in the St. Patrick's Day Parade. Hurray!

# A Surprise Visitor

When we got back to our house, we had a surprise visitor. I could hardly believe it. It was not a human visitor. It was a dog. He was sitting on our front stoop. As soon as he saw us, his tail started to wag.

"I wonder where he came from," I said to Andrew.

He did not look like any of the neighborhood dogs we knew.

"I never saw him before. But I like him," Andrew replied.

The dog was wearing a red collar. But I did not see any tags. His coat was short and curly. It was mostly black. Only his paws, his chest, and part of his face were gray. I knew they would be white if he had a bath. He was dirty. I could tell he was hungry, too.

"Mommy, Mommy!" I called. "Come outside!"

Mommy poked her head out the door. The dog turned to look at her. But he did not get up.

"Whose dog is that?" asked Mommy.

"We do not know," I replied.

"He was just sitting here," said Andrew.

Just then, Midgie poked her nose out the door. She started to sniff.

"Go back inside, Midgie," said Mommy. She gently shooed Midgie into the house.

"I think he is hungry," I said.

"We will get him some food," said Mommy. "And we will call the animal shelter to see if anyone has reported him missing."

We filled a bowl with some of Midgie's food. We filled another bowl with water. Andrew and I carried the bowls outside.

"Wow! Look at him eat," I said. "He really was hungry."

While the dog was gobbling up his food, Seth came home. He called the animal shelter. They had not heard anything about a missing black and white dog. But they took our phone number in case someone called them.

When the dog finished eating, Seth held his hand out to him. The dog sniffed it. Then he bumped his head against Seth's hand a few times.

"He wants you to pet him," I said.

"He looks like a friendly dog to me," Seth said. "We can let him sleep in the garage tonight. In the morning we will see if we can find his owner."

"I will get some towels to make a bed,"

I said. "And we have to leave him some water, too."

"I am sure you and Andrew will make a very nice home for him," said Mommy. "Just call Seth or me when it is ready."

I ran upstairs and got three raggedy old towels. I laid them one on top of the other in the garage. Then I set down a fresh bowl of water. Andrew gathered up some of Midgie's toys. (I do not think Midgie liked that very much.) He put them next to the towels.

When we were done, I got Seth.

"The guest room is ready," I said.

Seth used Midgie's leash to lead the dog to the garage. The dog knew right away that the bed was for him. He stepped onto it and circled around a few times. Then he lay down. He put his head on his paws and sighed.

"He is so cute!" I said. "But, wait. I want to get one more thing."

I ran inside the house and got two dog

biscuits. I put them next to the bowl of water in case our guest wanted a midnight snack.

"Good night," I said. "I am very glad you came to visit. If you need anything at all, just howl."

# Dog Found!

**O**n Saturday morning, I jumped out of bed and ran to Andrew's room.

"Are you up, Andrew? We have to feed the dog," I said.

"I am coming," Andrew replied.

We got dressed in a flash. We ran to the garage. The dog was sitting up on his bed. Both biscuits were gone. The bowl of water was almost empty. As soon as he saw us, the dog's tail began to wag.

"Good morning," I said. "I hope you had a good night's sleep."

The dog looked at me and turned his head to one side. He was gigundoly cute.

Andrew and I brought him food and more water. When he finished eating, he ran out of the garage. I thought he would just run off to find his home. But he did not. He poked around the yard awhile. (He needed to go to the bathroom.) Then he went right back into the garage.

Mommy and Seth came out to see the dog, too.

"It is time to start looking for this dog's owner," said Seth. "First we will make some signs."

"Hurray!" I said. I am a very good sign-maker.

"We will post them around the neighborhood," continued Seth.

"I will make some calls to see if anyone knows somebody who lost a dog," said Mommy. "And we can write an ad to put in the 'Lost and Found' section of the newspaper."

We all sat down together and decided

what to write for the poster and the ad.

"Let's print it in great big letters," I said. "That way everyone will read it."

We drew up the first one. The words jumped off the page. Anyone could see them from a mile away. That was just what we wanted.

```
Dog found!
Mostly black with white markings.
Red collar.
```

We added our phone number to the bottom of each sign. Then we made a dozen more.

Seth drove Andrew and me all around Stoneybrook. We took turns jumping out of the car and taping signs to trees and lampposts. We put them in stores and at the library and police station, too.

We were walking out of the library when Andrew said, "I really like that dog. I hope we can keep him."

"Do not get too attached to the dog, Andrew," I replied. "Remember what happens whenever we ask Mommy and Seth for a new pet."

"They say no," said Andrew. "But we did not ask for this pet. He just came along."

"He is not ours. And even if no one calls, I do not think they will let us keep him," I said.

I wanted the dog to be ours as much as Andrew did. But I was trying very hard to be grown-up. Sometimes that is what big sisters have to do.

# The Leprechaun

That afternoon Mr. Drucker called. He invited Andrew and me to a meeting of the Green Thumbs.

"It will be at my house tomorrow at three o'clock," said Mr. Drucker. "The parade director will be there. He would like to meet everyone who will be on the float."

We arrived at the Druckers' house right on time. Five grown-ups and six other kids were already there.

*Ding-dong!*

"That must be the director now," said Mr. Drucker.

When the door opened, a very unusual man walked into the room. First of all he was very, very small for a grown-up. He was not much taller than Andrew. He had a reddish beard and he was dressed all in green. He wore a funny hat with a round top and a curled-up brim. It was nothing like the hats that Daddy or Seth wear. Between his teeth was a green pipe with little people carved into the bowl. I tried not to stare too hard. I knew that was not polite.

The man began to speak. "A bright and shimmery day to you all," he said. "I am Patrick O'Casey, the director of the St. Paddy's Day parade."

Wow. Even his voice was unusual. It was much higher than other grown-up voices. And he had an accent. I think it was Irish.

"I would like to hear all about your float," said Mr. O'Casey. "Then I will answer questions about the glorious day that will soon be upon us."

"Our float will be in the shape of a flower box," said Mrs. Drucker. "We will wear green plant costumes."

"That is splendid!" said Mr. O'Casey. "Now let me tell you about the parade plan. We will meet at eleven-thirty on St. Patrick's Day outside the high school. You will be float number three."

While Mr. O'Casey answered questions, we were fitted for our costumes. Andrew and I were both going to be four-leaf clovers.

"Four-leaf clovers are lucky," I said to Andrew.

"Maybe we will get to keep the dog. That would be really lucky," Andrew replied.

"Now, if the grown-ups will excuse me, I would like to talk to the children for a spell," said Mr. O'Casey. "I have a secret for wee ears only."

Mr. O'Casey had a twinkle in his eye and a big smile on his face. I wiggled my way up close so I could hear. I just love secrets.

When we were gathered around him,

27

Mr. O'Casey whispered, "I am a leprechaun. A leprechaun is a real and true fairy."

Andrew's eyes opened wide and his mouth dropped open. "Like the tooth fairy?" he asked.

"Why, yes, I suppose so," said Mr. O'Casey.

He told us that he came from a long line of leprechauns who fixed the shoes of dancing fairies.

"Leprechauns keep pots of gold hidden away in special places. To find the gold, you have to travel all the way to the end of a rainbow," he whispered.

Then he asked us to close our eyes and count to ten. When we opened them again, he was gone!

That day Andrew could not stop talking about Mr. O'Casey. He truly believed that Mr. O'Casey was a leprechaun. All the little kids did.

I wanted to believe it, too. I believe in elves and fairies and things. And here was a grown-up who *said* he was leprechaun. So it had to be true.

This was very exciting. I wanted to know everything about leprechauns. I could hardly wait to see Mr. O'Casey again. But first I had to tell Nancy the news.

# Fetch

I went to Nancy's house right after the meeting.

"You will never guess who I met!" I said. "The parade director's name is Mr. O'Casey. He says he is a real and true leprechaun."

I told Nancy everything I could remember. I told her what he wore and how he talked. I told her about the pots of gold.

"He said they are hidden at the end of a rainbow. I wonder how you get to the end of a rainbow."

"This is amazing," said Nancy. "Could Mr. O'Casey *really* be a leprechaun?"

"I do not know," I replied. "But I do know he is not like any other grown-up I have ever met."

"I am not so sure a real leprechaun would live in Stoneybrook," said Nancy.

"I have an idea," I said. "There is going to be another parade meeting next weekend. You could come with Andrew and me. You could meet Mr. O'Casey yourself."

"We can decide together if he is telling the truth," Nancy replied. "And I just remembered I have a book we could look at. It is all about fairies and elves. Maybe there will be a picture of a leprechaun in it."

Nancy found the book buried under a pile on her bookcase. We turned every page. But we did not find a picture of a leprechaun.

"Boo," I said. "That would have solved our mystery for sure. Oh, well. We will wait for next weekend. We will find out more then. Do you want to come over now and play with the dog?"

"Sure," replied Nancy.

Nancy loves dogs. She wishes she could get one. But she already has a kitten, Pokey. And her parents do not want another pet.

The dog was sitting on his bed in the garage. I found a stick and threw it across the yard.

"Fetch!" I said.

The dog leaped up and ran after the stick. He brought it to me. I threw it again. The dog ran after it again. This time he brought it to Nancy. Nancy threw it and the dog fetched it again.

"Can I play, too?" asked Andrew.

The dog dropped the stick at Andrew's feet. We all laughed.

"I guess that means yes!" said Andrew.

"Has anyone called to ask about the dog?" asked Nancy.

"Yes, a few people called. But none of

them turned out to be his owner," I replied.

I was kind of glad. I knew it would be nice for him to be with his owner again. But I was not ready to say good-bye to him. I liked having him around.

# Can We Keep Him?

No one called about the dog on Monday. No one called on Tuesday. No one called on Wednesday.

I started to feel sorry for the dog. He was sleeping in the garage all by himself. He probably missed the people he used to live with. Even though we were being very nice to him.

At dinner on Thursday I said, "I am surprised no one is calling anymore about the dog. He is so sweet. And our posters are all over town."

"He might have wandered away from another town," said Seth. "Then his owners would not have seen the posters."

Just then the phone rang. Mommy answered it. I thought it was going to be my friend, Hannie. But it was not.

"Yes, we did find a dog," Mommy said into the phone.

She listened for a minute then said, "Yes, the dog's coat is kind of curly. And, yes, all four paws are white."

Oh no! This was it. The dog's owner was calling to claim him. I had told Andrew not to get too attached to the dog. I had told myself, too. But I do not think I listened to myself. I felt like crying.

Then I heard Mommy say, "Your dog's name is Bessie? Oh, I am very sorry. This cannot be your dog then. The dog is a male."

Mommy said good-bye and hung up the phone.

"Yes!!!" cried Andrew and I at the same time.

Before I could stop him, Andrew asked the question I had told him not to ask.

"Can we keep him?" he said.

I kicked Andrew under the table. Then I heard something amazing. I heard Seth say, "Well, why not? It is not as though we went out looking for a dog. He found us."

"He *is* sweet," said Mommy. "He *does* need a home. And you kids *have* been good about taking care of him."

"So can we keep him?" asked Andrew again.

This time I did not kick Andrew under the table. Instead I crossed my fingers and hoped Mommy and Seth would say yes. Do you know what? They did!

"We must all understand that his owner could still show up and claim him. We have to be ready to give him up," said Mommy.

"Okay. But can we bring him inside the house now?" I asked. "He will be so happy."

"Rocky and Midgie are upstairs. So this

is a good time to let him explore his new home," said Seth.

Yippee!! Andrew and I raced each other out to the garage. As soon as the dog saw us, his tail began to wag. It was wagging faster than usual. He must have known we had good news for him.

"Come in," I said. "Come and see your new home."

The dog followed us into the house. Seth had put a gate up at the bottom of the stairs so the dog would stay on the first floor. Right away, the dog started sniffing everything in sight.

Suddenly I realized something important. We did not know the dog's name.

"What should we call him?" I said.

We tried out a whole bunch of names. Moe. Jack. Buddy. Wags. Boy.

Then Andrew said, "I want to call him Lucky!"

I wished I had thought of that name. It was perfect. We were lucky we found him on our stoop. We were lucky we were getting to keep him. And he was lucky he had a new family to love him.

I told Andrew I liked that name a lot. So did Mommy and Seth.

"Lucky, come!" I said.

He trotted right over to me. I guess he liked his new name, too.

# Crash! Bam! Kaboom!

**W**e played with Lucky until it was time for bed. When I fell asleep, I dreamed he was on the Green Thumb float with Andrew and me. Lucky was wearing a four-leaf clover costume just like ours.

*CRASH! BAM! KABOOM!*

I sat straight up in my bed. I was not dreaming anymore. But I wished I was. Something terrible was happening downstairs.

In a flash, Mommy was in my room. Then Seth came in with Andrew. Seth was carrying Andrew's baseball bat.

*CRASH! KABOOM!*

"You three stay here," said Seth. "We may have a burglar. I will look downstairs. I will tell you if you need to call nine-one-one."

He walked out of my room clutching Andrew's bat.

"You kids stay here," said Mommy. "I do not want Seth to go downstairs alone."

She left carrying my skateboard. Maybe she planned to skate into the burglar and trip him. Or else she would bop him on the head with it.

Then I got an idea.

"You stay here," I said to Andrew.

I knew Mommy and Seth would be mad at me for leaving the room. But I could not let Mommy go out there alone.

I grabbed my umbrella. If that burglar knew what was good for him, he would run away. Otherwise I would poke him in the belly.

"Hey, wait for me!" said Andrew.

The four of us tiptoed down the stairs in a line. Watch out, burglar. Here we come! *CRASH! BAM! KABOOM!*

Two bodies went speeding through the living room. Only they were not burglar bodies. They were furry bodies. One belonged to Lucky. The other belonged to Rocky.

"What a relief!" said Seth.

"But look at our living room," said Mommy. "It is wrecked."

Suddenly the chase stopped. Rocky was nowhere in sight. Lucky was looking around the room. He was shaking.

"Lucky must be afraid of Rocky," I said.

"I thought cats were supposed to be scared of dogs," said Andrew.

"Sometimes it is the other way around," said Seth.

"Watch out!" I cried. "Rocky is back."

Rocky sneaked out from behind the couch. *Meowrr!!!* He started chasing Lucky again.

"We have to help Lucky," I said. "He is too scared!"

"Rocky, scat!" said Seth. He stamped his foot on the floor. Rocky turned and headed into the kitchen. Seth followed him. He put down a bowl of water for him. Then he closed the door.

"He will be okay in there for the night," said Seth.

"Hey, where is Midgie?" asked Andrew.

"Midgie is a scaredy dog," said Mommy. "As soon as she heard the noise, she ran under our bed to hide."

"Speaking of bed, it is time for us to go back upstairs and get some sleep," said Seth.

He put the gate back up. (Rocky must have knocked it down when he jumped over it.)

I went back to my room and snuggled under the covers. I hoped I would not dream about furry burglars.

# I Told You So

We had another meeting of the Green Thumbs on Sunday. I decided it was time to get into the St. Patrick's Day spirit. So I wore a bright green ribbon in my hair.

Andrew and I stopped to pick up Nancy on our way to the Druckers' house.

"I am a little nervous," said Nancy. "What if Mr. O'Casey turns out to be a real leprechaun? I never met a real leprechaun before. I might not know what to say."

"Do not worry," I replied. "Even if he is a real leprechaun, he is a friendly one."

"He *is* a lepicon. He *is*," said Andrew.

"We are not so sure," I said. "Nancy and I will tell you later if we think he is a real leprechaun or not."

When we reached the Druckers' house, I introduced Nancy to everyone.

"Thank you for letting me come to your meeting," said Nancy.

"We are happy to have you here," said Mrs. Drucker. "As I always say, the more the merrier."

"You can even join us in the parade if you want," said Mr. Drucker.

"Thank you very much," replied Nancy politely. "But I do not think so."

Nancy told me later that she would rather watch a parade than be in it. That is not like me at all. I want to be in everything!

"Karen and Andrew, come try on your costumes," said Mrs. Harris. (Mrs. Harris lives next door to the Druckers.)

She held the four-leaf clover costume up for me to see.

"Oh, it is beautiful!" I said. I ran to the bathroom to try it on.

"Ta-daa!" I said when I came out.

"Oh my," said Mrs. Harris. "I think it needs a little work."

When I looked down I could tell that one side was a lot longer than the other. I was a lopsided four-leaf clover. I tipped to one side to even it out.

Just then, Mr. O'Casey walked in.

"The luck of the Irish be with us!" he cried when he saw me. "I am sure it will turn out just fine."

Nancy tugged on one of my lopsided leaves.

"Can you introduce me now?" she whispered.

"Um, Mr. O'Casey, I would like you to meet my friend, Nancy," I said.

"I am glad to meet such a fine girl as you," he replied. Then he whispered, "Tell me, Nancy, have you ever met a real live leprechaun before?"

Nancy was tongue-tied. She shook her head to say no.

Andrew tried on his costume next. It was lopsided, too. Mrs. Harris promised to have them both ready in time for the St. Patrick's parade.

Mr. O'Casey checked all the costumes. Then he asked the kids to gather round him again. He wanted to tell us another story.

"Once upon a time there was a mischievous leprechaun. He liked to sneak from house to house, stealing gold coins wherever he could. And you know where he put them all, don't you?" asked Mr. O'Casey.

I waved my hand and called out, "At the end of a rainbow?"

"That is right," said Mr. O'Casey.

I wanted to ask exactly how a person could travel to the end of the rainbow. But it was time to go.

On the way home, Nancy said, "You

know, I think Mr. O'Casey just might be a real leprechaun."

"I think so, too," I replied.

Andrew smiled. "I told you so. I told you so!" he said.

# Hiss and Growl

As soon as we got home, Andrew and I took Lucky for a walk. We were trying our best to take good care of him. After all, he was our very own dog.

Lucky loved going for walks. Sometimes he got excited and pulled us. Then Andrew and I had to hold onto the leash together.

We walked up our street and down.

"It is time to go home, Lucky. It is time for your dinner," I said.

When we walked into the house, Rocky was waiting by the door. *Hiss!*

"Rocky, scat!" I said.

I shooed Rocky into the den. I went back into the living room.

"Okay, Lucky. You can have your dinner now," I said.

But Lucky was not there. I went into the kitchen. Andrew was filling a bowl with food. But Lucky was not there either.

I went upstairs. I found Lucky curled up on my bed. He was resting his chin on Goosie's lap. I gave him a hug.

"I am sorry Rocky is picking on you," I said.

I led Lucky back to the kitchen. Andrew put down the bowl of food. I put down a bowl of fresh water. Lucky trotted over to his dinner.

The door opened and Midgie raced in. *Grrr!*

"Midgie, no!" I said.

I scooted Midgie out of the kitchen. Poor Lucky. Rocky hissed whenever Lucky walked by. Midgie growled whenever he went near her food or toys or water. And it was hard to keep them apart in the same house.

Lucky took one look at his bowl and turned his head away. I guess he had lost his appetite. I would lose mine, too, if someone growled at me every time I tried to eat.

"Let's take his dinner to the yard. Lucky can have a picnic," I said. "You hold Midgie while we go outside."

I grabbed Lucky's food and headed out the door.

"Make sure Midgie stays . . ."

Uh-oh. Too late. There was a squirrel in the yard. Lucky raced out the door after the squirrel. Midgie got away from Andrew and raced after Lucky. I raced out the door after Midgie. Andrew raced out the door after me.

We all ran around the yard twice. Finally the squirrel dashed up a tree. That left Lucky, Midgie, Andrew, and me. We ran in circles around the yard. The squirrel was sitting on a branch watching us. (I think I heard him laughing.)

Mommy and Seth came outside. All six of us raced around the yard. Finally Seth caught Midgie. Mommy caught Lucky.

"We've got a problem," Seth said.

A black and white and furry problem, I thought.

# Family Talk

We put Rocky and Midgie in one room. We put Lucky in another. Then we sat down together in the living room.

"It is time for a family talk," said Mommy. "We have to decide what to do about our pet situation."

"We all know that Lucky is a good dog," said Seth.

"Then why don't Rocky and Midgie like him?" asked Andrew.

"I don't know," said Seth. "But my guess is that Rocky and Midgie feel threatened by Lucky."

"But Lucky is so sweet. He would never hurt them," I said.

"Rocky and Midgie are getting old. They do not want to take any chances. Also, they do not want to share their things. They do not like Lucky being around their food, their toys, or even us," said Seth.

"That is not very nice," said Andrew. "In school we learn that we should share."

"Let's see if we can find a way to solve the problems," said Seth. "We are going to do our best to keep Lucky."

I did not even want to think about giving Lucky up. I needed to think of something fast.

"We can keep them apart all the time," I said.

"It is a good plan. But we are not very good at making it work," said Mommy.

"Can Lucky live in the garage again?" asked Andrew.

"He was too lonely there," I said. Then I had a brainstorm. "How about this! We could build a dog house for Lucky. We could put it in my room and he could live there all the time. Then we could make a slide from my window to the yard. When Lucky wanted to go out he would bark. I would open the window. He would slide down. How about that?"

This sounded like an excellent idea to me. I felt gigundoly proud.

"How would he get back up?" asked Andrew.

"Hmm. That is a good question," I said. "I know! We would put him in a basket and pull him back up."

"It is a great idea," said Mommy. "But it would be an awful lot of work for everyone. Including Lucky."

Boo and bullfrogs. I was out of ideas. I knew what was coming next.

"I am sad to say this, but keeping Lucky is just too difficult," said Seth. "I think the best thing for everyone would be to find him a new home."

"It will have to be a very, very good

home," I said. "We cannot just put him anywhere."

I could feel my bottom lip shaking a little. That happened whenever I tried not to cry.

"I promise you we will not give up Lucky until we find a good home," said Mommy.

"Is it okay if we take Lucky out to the yard now to play?" I asked.

"Of course," said Seth. "I will make sure Midgie and Rocky do not get out again."

Andrew and I went out to the yard with Lucky. While we played fetch with him, we thought of a plan.

"Here is what we will do," I said. "Tomorrow after school we will take Lucky around the neighborhood. Once people see him, someone will want him for sure."

"We should give him a bath first. He is dirty," said Andrew.

"You are right. We will give Lucky a bath. We will make him look extra beautiful," I said. "Then we will find the perfect home for him. I just know we will."

# Would You Like
# This Dog?

"Be careful. We do not want to get any soap in his eyes," I said.

It was Monday afternoon. Andrew and I were giving Lucky his bath. He was such a good dog. He did not try to jump out of the tub or anything.

We rinsed him off carefully. Mommy said it is important to get all the soap out. If you leave any in, dogs get itchy. We did not want Lucky going around scratching. People would think he had fleas. No one wants a dog with fleas.

We dried him off with a towel. Then we used the hair dryer. We did not want him going out wet and catching a cold. No one wants a dog with a drippy nose.

"Let's put a ribbon in his hair," I said.

"No way," said Andrew. "He is a boy dog. Boys do not wear ribbons."

He was probably right.

"How about hanging a four-leaf clover from his neck?" I said. "Lots of people will want him if they think he really is a lucky dog."

That sounded okay to Andrew. I cut a four-leaf clover out of green construction paper. I hung it on a piece of string and put it around Lucky's neck.

He looked so handsome. I wished we did not have to give him away. But we had no choice. We clipped on his leash and set out to find a new home for Lucky.

It was a bright, warm day. March was finally turning into a lamb just like Ms. Colman said it would. I was glad it was not snowy and sloppy. No one wants a sloppy dog.

We walked up the street and knocked on the doors of the families we know. We are not allowed to go to any house unless we know the family who lives there. (We skipped Nancy's house. I knew she could not take Lucky.)

First we tried Bobby Gianelli's house. Since he is not a bully anymore we could let him have Lucky.

"Would you like to adopt Lucky?" I asked. "He is our dog. But we cannot keep him."

"He looks like a neat dog," said Bobby. "But my dad is allergic to dogs. That is why we cannot have one."

"Too bad," I said.

We tried Mrs. Harris's house. This time Andrew asked if she would like to adopt Lucky.

"No, thank you," she said. "You see, I am a cat person. I have six cats."

"Can't a cat person be a dog person, too?" asked Andrew when we left.

"Why not?" I replied. "Both our families

have cats and dogs in the same house."

We tried Kathryn's and Willie's house next. They were out with their mom. But their dad was home.

"I am really sorry we cannot take him. Mrs. Barnes is afraid of dogs," he said.

"No one could be scared of Lucky. He is the sweetest dog in the world," I said.

"I can see that," replied Mr. Barnes. "But I know it would not work out."

"Maybe you should take him for the afternoon. Maybe Mrs. Barnes would like him," I said.

"Thank you anyway," said Mr. Barnes. "But we cannot take Lucky."

We went from house to house to house. Everyone said that Lucky was a sweet and beautiful dog. But no one wanted to adopt him.

Could it be that Lucky was not so lucky after all?

# The Rainbow

There was one more meeting of the Green Thumbs on Wednesday afternoon. We tried on our costumes again. They were all fixed. So we got to take them home.

Thursday passed quickly. Friday passed quickly. When I woke up on Saturday, it was St. Patrick's Day!

I looked out the window. Darn. It was raining. Ms. Colman had not said anything about March being like a fish. Oh, well. Mr. O'Casey said the parade was going to be held rain or shine.

I got up and got dressed. This is what I wore: green shirt, new green leggings, green socks, and a green ribbon in my hair. (I wished I had green underwear, too.)

I kept Midgie and Rocky out of the kitchen while I fed Lucky his breakfast. Then I ate mine. When I had finished, I went back upstairs to try on my costume again.

I looked out the window to see if it was still raining. I saw that it had stopped. That was not all I saw.

"Mommy! Seth! Andrew! Hurry!" I called.

"What is it?" cried Mommy. "Are you all right?"

"I am fine," I said. "Just look. There is a rainbow!" I pointed to it as if I had put it there myself.

"Let's go outside," said Seth. "We will be able to see it better."

The four of us stood in the middle of the yard looking up. (Lucky was living in the

garage again. He came out to look at the rainbow, too.)

"Ooh," said Andrew.

"Ahh," said Seth.

"I will be right back," said Mommy. She ran inside and came back with her camera. Mommy pointed her camera at the sky.

"Hey, rainbow! Smile!" I said.

While Mommy was taking pictures, I started thinking. Today was St. Patrick's Day. And there was a rainbow in the sky. I decided this had to be a sign. This must be the leprechaun's rainbow. That meant there was gold hidden at the end of it. I had to go there. I just had to. I was *sure* to find a pot of gold if I did.

"I am going to Nancy's house," I said. "I will be right back."

I ran next door and rang Nancy's bell. I wanted to tell her about the rainbow. I wanted to ask her to come with me to look for the gold. But no one was home.

When I got back to my house, everyone was inside again. I did not think it would

take too long to get to the end of the rainbow and back. So I decided not to tell anyone that I was going. They might think that
looking for a leprechaun's gold was foolish.

I wheeled my bike out of the garage and
pointed it toward the rainbow.

# Follow That Rainbow

I rode down my street. I rode and rode and rode. I could not understand why the rainbow did not seem to be getting any closer. I pedaled faster. I had to reach the rainbow before it disappeared.

I was so busy thinking about finding the end of the rainbow that I did not realize how far I had ridden. I was way past where I am allowed to be. I am not allowed to go more than five blocks in any direction. I know every house on those five blocks.

I had passed those houses a long time ago.

I decided it was too late to turn around. So I kept on pedaling. I saw houses and blocks I had never seen before. Not even driving in the car. I wondered if I had pedaled right out of Stoneybrook. I felt a little scared so far from home.

Then the strangest thing happened. I started seeing houses I knew again. Only they were not houses from my little-house neighborhood. They were houses from my big-house neighborhood. Wow. I had ridden awfully far.

I pedaled into Stoneybrook Playground. I saw our swings and our slides and our hopscotch boxes. I had helped build the playground. Nearly everyone in Stoneybrook had helped. We had raised the money and built it ourselves. I was very glad to see it now.

I was tired from all that pedaling. I thought about sitting down and taking a

rest. But I knew I could not stop. The rainbow was still ahead of me. The end seemed to be just past a wooded area.

I leaned my bike against the playground fence and headed into woods. I walked a little way. Then I started to run. I had come so far. I did not want to miss the rainbow now.

I ran farther and farther into the woods. The farther I went, the darker it got. When I looked up I could not see the rainbow anymore. I turned around and around and around.

Uh-oh. I still could not find the end of the rainbow. And now I had no idea which way was home. I was lost.

# The Ride Home

I remembered what Ms. Colman had said to do in an emergency. She had said to keep calm. I took a deep breath. Then I looked around me. I could see my footprints pretty clearly. I had followed a path through the woods. All I had to do was follow it back the way I had come.

Okay, footprints, I thought. Lead me home. I followed my footprints a little way. Then they disappeared. The ground was still muddy from the rain. But I could tell I was on a path. And I knew I was heading in the right direction. So I kept on going.

I ran and ran. Finally I saw the swings and slides again. Hurray! I was out of breath. But I had made it.

I looked at my watch. Yikes. It was late. I was so, so tired. All I wanted to do was sit down and rest. But I had been gone so long. I knew my family would probably be worried. There was no time to lose. I jumped on my bike and began the ride home.

All of a sudden, I heard someone calling my name.

"Karen! Hey, Karen! What are you doing here?"

It was Kristy. She was taking Emily for a ride on the back of her bike.

I usually tell Kristy everything. But I did not feel like telling her how I ended up all the way at the playground. I did not want her to know that I had been looking for a pot of gold at the end of a rainbow.

So all I said was, "I was riding my bike. I guess I rode too far."

"You sure did. You know you are not supposed to go more than five blocks from either house," replied Kristy. "Come on. I will ride back with you to the little house."

"It is okay," I said. "I can get back by myself."

I only said that because I did not want to look like a big baby. But I really was not so sure I could find my way home again. I hoped Kristy would insist on coming with me. She did. What a relief.

It took a long time to get home. I could hardly believe I had ridden so far by myself. I saw the houses that were five blocks away from the little house. Then four blocks. Then two blocks. Finally I saw the little house.

"Thank you, Kristy!" I said cheerfully. "You can go home now."

"No way," said Kristy. "I am taking you right to your door."

# Tricked

"Karen, where have you been?" cried Mommy. "We were worried sick about you."

Mommy was upset. I was not too surprised.

"We were about to call the police," said Seth. "You told us you were going to Nancy's house. Then Nancy called. We found out she had not seen you all morning."

"Where did you go?" asked Andrew. Even he sounded worried.

"I went for a ride," I said. "I got a little lost."

"I found Karen all the way over near Stoneybrook Playground," said Kristy.

"Thank you for riding home with her," said Mommy. "Would you or Emily like a drink? Can we drive you back to your house?"

"No, thank you," said Kristy. "We are fine. But we really should get back. 'Bye, Karen. I will wave to you at the parade."

(I had called my big-house family and told them to look for me on the Green Thumbs float.)

" 'Bye," I said. "Oh, I almost forgot. Happy St. Patrick's Day."

"You cannot just ride off without telling anyone you are leaving," said Mommy after Kristy and Emily had left. "And you know very well you are not supposed to ride more than five blocks from the house. We will have to discuss your punishment. But we will do it later. If we do not leave soon, we will be late for the parade."

I put my bike back in the garage. Then I went upstairs and put on my four-leaf clover costume. It was not bringing me much luck. It was not lucky that I had gotten lost. And it was not lucky that I was going to be punished.

On the way to the high school, Seth said, "I am curious, Karen. Will you please tell me where on earth you thought you were going?"

I decided I owed everyone an explanation. After all, I had really worried them. So I said, "I was going to look for a pot of gold at the end of the rainbow."

"Oh, Karen, honey. What made you think you could find gold at the end of the rainbow?" asked Mommy.

"Mr. O'Casey told us they are hidden there. He is the parade director. And he is a leprechaun. He knows these things," I replied.

"But leprechauns are not real people. They are made up. Mr. O'Casey was just telling you a story," said Mommy.

"No!" said Andrew. "He is a lepicon. He told us so."

Maybe Andrew still believed Mr. O'Casey. But I did not. I was sure Mommy was telling us the truth. There are no such things as leprechauns. I had known it all along. But he had tricked me.

I was gigundoly mad at Mr. O'Casey.

# The Parade

By the time we reached the high school, a huge crowd was there. I had never seen so much green in my life.

"Karen, take my hand. Andrew, hold onto Seth," said Mommy. "We have to hurry. And we do not want anyone getting lost."

We started weaving in and out of the crowd looking for the Green Thumbs float. On the way we ran into Mr. O'Casey. He was wearing a leprechaun costume. But now I knew the truth. He was not a leprechaun. He was just a short grown-up dressed in green.

"Oh, for the love of St. Paddy! Don't you kids look grand," he said.

I refused to look at Mr. O'Casey. I looked down at my feet instead.

"Could you please point us in the direction of the Green Thumbs float?" asked Seth.

Before he had a chance to answer, Andrew interrupted.

"Do you know what? Karen went to look for a pot of gold this morning. And she got lost. And Mommy says there are no such things as lepicons," said Andrew.

(Leave it to him to spill the beans.)

"Oh, my. Did you really go looking for gold, Karen?" asked Mr. O'Casey.

"Yes, I did," I replied. "I tried to get to the end of the rainbow. That is where you said the gold would be. But I got lost and everyone was worried about me. And now I am going to be punished. And you are not even a leprechaun. You tricked us!"

I was out of breath from talking so fast.

"I feel terrible," said Mr. O'Casey. "You are right. I am not really a leprechaun. Leprechauns do not exist. But I did not mean to *trick* you or the other children. I only told you those stories because I thought you would enjoy them."

I did not care what Mr. O'Casey said. I was still mad at him. I went back to looking at my feet.

"Come along," Mr. O'Casey said to Seth. "I will lead you to your float."

He walked with us until we could see the float. Then he said good-bye.

"Hello, Karen! Hello, Andrew!"

Mr. Drucker was calling to us from the float. I tried to smile. After all, it was not Mr. Drucker's fault that we had been tricked.

He helped us up. We stood with the other kids who were dressed as four-leaf clovers. If I had not been in such a bad mood I would have been having fun.

I looked for Nancy and my big-house

family. But I could not find them in the crowd. Maybe I would see them when the float started moving.

"Welcome, everyone! Welcome to Stoneybrook's St. Patrick's Day parade! I am Mr. O'Casey, the parade director."

Mr. O'Casey was standing at the top of the steps in front of the school. He was talking into a microphone. I put my hands over my ears so I would not have to listen to him. The next thing I knew, our float was moving. We rode through the streets into the middle of town.

A marching band played a song I knew called "Danny Boy." Lots of people were wearing green hats, and buttons that said, "Kiss Me, I'm Irish." One man had dyed his eyebrows and mustache green.

Everyone seemed to be having a good time except me. I knew I was going to be punished as soon as I got home from the parade.

# A Present

Mommy and Seth met Andrew and me after the parade. I was gigundoly tired from chasing rainbows and being grumpy. I did not say one word on the way home.

I knew the only thing that would cheer me up was seeing Lucky. So I went to the garage to visit him.

"Please do not stay out there too long," said Mommy. "We need to talk."

"Lucky, did you hear what happened to me today?" I said.

I told him the whole sad story. You know

what he did? He listened to me. Then he licked my nose. It tickled. What a great dog!

"I will find you the best home ever. You just leave it to me," I said. "I wish we could visit longer. But I have to go inside now. I have to find out what my punishment is going to be. See you later."

Mommy and Seth came up to my room to talk with me.

"You broke two important rules, Karen," said Mommy. "First you went off without telling us you were leaving. Then you went too far from home."

"You know we do not make these rules to be mean. We make them to keep you safe," said Seth.

"All right. Now for your punishment," said Mommy. "You may not ride your bicycle for two weeks starting today. Is that understood?"

I could feel my bottom lip start to shake. I knew I could not talk. If I did I would cry. So I just nodded.

"I am sorry this has been such a difficult day for you," said Seth.

After they left I did not feel like crying anymore. I felt like yelling. I felt like yelling at Mr. O'Casey. This was all his fault.

I was mad for three whole days.

Then a package came for me in the mail. I wondered if it was a present from one of my grandparents. But it was not my birthday. I looked at the return address. Guess who it was from. Mr. O'Casey. I thought about sending it back unopened. But I was too curious. What could it be?

I opened the box. On top was a letter.

DEAR KAREN,
I AM SO SORRY THAT MY STORIES UPSET YOU. I SHOULD NOT HAVE LED YOU TO BELIEVE I WAS TRULY A LEP-RECHAUN WHEN I AM NOT.

I AM SENDING YOU THIS CHARM TO BRING YOU GOOD LUCK.
                    YOUR FRIEND (I HOPE),
                    MR. O'CASEY

There was a white box underneath some tissue paper. I opened it and found a tiny glass ball with a four-leaf clover inside it. I could not stop looking at my present. It was beautiful.

# Lucky's New Home

DEAR MR. O'CASEY,
THANK YOU FOR THE BEAUTIFUL
GOOD LUCK CHARM. IT WAS VERY
~~THOTFUL~~ NICE OF YOU TO SEND IT.
I AM SORRY I WAS SO MEAN AT THE
PARADE. I WAS VERY MAD AT YOU.
BUT I KNOW NOW THAT YOU DID NOT
TELL THOSE STORIES TO TRICK US.
PLEASE WRITE BACK SOON.
YOUR FRIEND,
KAREN

DEAR KAREN,

DO NOT WORRY ABOUT BEING MAD AT ME. I AM JUST GLAD WE ARE FRIENDS NOW. IT IS ALWAYS NICE TO HAVE NEW FRIENDS. ESPECIALLY FOR SOMEONE WHO LIVES ALONE LIKE ME. SOMETIMES I GET LONELY.

I HOPE YOU WILL WRITE BACK FROM TIME TO TIME.

YOUR FRIEND,
MR. O'CASEY

DEAR MR. O'CASEY,

DID YOU SAY YOU GET LONELY SOMETIMES? I HAVE A REALLY GREAT IDEA. IT COULD HELP YOU. FIRST I NEED TO KNOW A FEW THINGS. WHAT KIND OF HOUSE DO YOU LIVE IN? WHAT KINDS OF THINGS DO YOU LIKE TO DO?

PLEASE WRITE BACK REALLY SOON!

YOUR FRIEND,
KAREN

P.S. DO YOU LIKE ANIMALS?

90

DEAR KAREN,

I LOVE ANIMALS! HOW ABOUT YOU?
HERE ARE THE ANSWERS TO YOUR
QUESTIONS. I LIVE IN A WHITE HOUSE
WITH GREEN SHUTTERS. I HAVE A BIG
YARD WITH A FENCE ALL AROUND IT.
I LIKE TO SIT IN THE YARD AND READ
WHEN THE WEATHER IS NICE. I LIKE
TO TAKE LONG WALKS. I LIKE TO RENT
MOVIES.

I HOPE YOU WILL TELL ME YOUR
IDEA SOON.

YOUR FRIEND,
MR. O'CASEY

DEAR MR. O'CASEY,

HERE IS MY IDEA. I THINK YOU
SHOULD HAVE A DOG. ANDREW AND
I FOUND ONE ON OUR STOOP. WE
NAMED HIM LUCKY. WE CANNOT
KEEP HIM BECAUSE OUR OTHER PETS
ARE MEAN TO HIM.

YOU HAVE A HOUSE AND A YARD.
YOU LIKE TO TAKE WALKS. YOU ARE
A NICE PERSON. LUCKY WOULD BE
LUCKY TO LIVE WITH YOU. YOU
WOULD BE LUCKY TOO BECAUSE YOU
WOULD NOT HAVE TO BE LONELY
ANYMORE.
    PLEASE WRITE BACK SOON.
                    YOUR FRIEND,
                    KAREN


DEAR KAREN,
    I LOVE YOUR IDEA! I WILL COME
MEET LUCKY NEXT SATURDAY AT
THREE.
                    YOUR FRIEND,
                    MR. O'CASEY


DEAR MR. O'CASEY,
    HOW IS LUCKY? IS HE HAPPY? ARE
YOU HAVING A GOOD TIME? PLEASE
WRITE BACK SOON.
                    YOUR FRIEND,
                    KAREN

92

Dear Karen,

Thank you so much for giving me Lucky. He is happy in his new home. And I am happy to have him.

We play in the yard. We take long walks together. And now I have someone to tell my stories to. Thanks to you and Lucky, I am not so lonely anymore.

Your friend,
Mr. O'Casey

## About the Author

ANN M. MARTIN lives in New York City and loves animals, especially cats. She has two cats of her own, Mouse and Rosie.

Other books by Ann M. Martin that you might enjoy are *Stage Fright*; *Me and Katie (the Pest)*; and the books in *The Baby-sitters Club* series.

Ann likes ice cream and *I Love Lucy*. And she has her own little sister, whose name is Jane.

# Little Sister

Don't miss #60

## KAREN'S PONY

Mr. Macdonell rounded up the goat and the chickens and shooed them into the van. That left just the pony. The poor old pony. Now he was all alone.

As the van was pulling out of the yard, I heard Mr. Macdonell say to Mrs. Macdonell, "I wish we could sell the pony, too. If no one buys him, we will have to take him to the shelter."

"Daddy! Daddy would you come here, please?" I called.

"What is it, Karen?" asked Daddy.

I explained to him about the pony. I explained how he was all alone.

"And if no one buys him, he will have to go to the shelter," I said.

"Hmm," said Daddy.

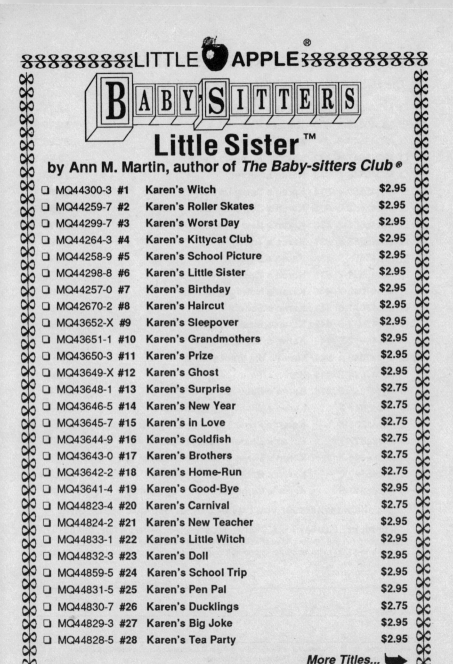

# LITTLE APPLE ®

# B·A·B·Y·S·I·T·T·E·R·S

## Little Sister ™

### by Ann M. Martin, author of *The Baby-sitters Club* ®

| | | | |
|---|---|---|---|
| ❑ | MQ44300-3 | #1 | Karen's Witch | $2.95 |
| ❑ | MQ44259-7 | #2 | Karen's Roller Skates | $2.95 |
| ❑ | MQ44299-7 | #3 | Karen's Worst Day | $2.95 |
| ❑ | MQ44264-3 | #4 | Karen's Kittycat Club | $2.95 |
| ❑ | MQ44258-9 | #5 | Karen's School Picture | $2.95 |
| ❑ | MQ44298-8 | #6 | Karen's Little Sister | $2.95 |
| ❑ | MQ44257-0 | #7 | Karen's Birthday | $2.95 |
| ❑ | MQ42670-2 | #8 | Karen's Haircut | $2.95 |
| ❑ | MQ43652-X | #9 | Karen's Sleepover | $2.95 |
| ❑ | MQ43651-1 | #10 | Karen's Grandmothers | $2.95 |
| ❑ | MQ43650-3 | #11 | Karen's Prize | $2.95 |
| ❑ | MQ43649-X | #12 | Karen's Ghost | $2.95 |
| ❑ | MQ43648-1 | #13 | Karen's Surprise | $2.75 |
| ❑ | MQ43646-5 | #14 | Karen's New Year | $2.75 |
| ❑ | MQ43645-7 | #15 | Karen's in Love | $2.75 |
| ❑ | MQ43644-9 | #16 | Karen's Goldfish | $2.75 |
| ❑ | MQ43643-0 | #17 | Karen's Brothers | $2.75 |
| ❑ | MQ43642-2 | #18 | Karen's Home-Run | $2.75 |
| ❑ | MQ43641-4 | #19 | Karen's Good-Bye | $2.95 |
| ❑ | MQ44823-4 | #20 | Karen's Carnival | $2.75 |
| ❑ | MQ44824-2 | #21 | Karen's New Teacher | $2.95 |
| ❑ | MQ44833-1 | #22 | Karen's Little Witch | $2.95 |
| ❑ | MQ44832-3 | #23 | Karen's Doll | $2.95 |
| ❑ | MQ44859-5 | #24 | Karen's School Trip | $2.95 |
| ❑ | MQ44831-5 | #25 | Karen's Pen Pal | $2.95 |
| ❑ | MQ44830-7 | #26 | Karen's Ducklings | $2.75 |
| ❑ | MQ44829-3 | #27 | Karen's Big Joke | $2.95 |
| ❑ | MQ44828-5 | #28 | Karen's Tea Party | $2.95 |

*More Titles...* ➡️